Topsy and Tim
The New Baby

By Jean and Gareth Adamson

Illustrations by Belinda Worsley

A catalogue record for this book is available from the British Library

This title was previously published as part of the Topsy and Tim Learnabout series
Published by Ladybird Books Ltd
A Penguin Company
Penguin Books Ltd., 80 Strand, London WC2R 0RL, UK
Penguin Books Australia Ltd., Camberwell, Victoria, Australia
Penguin Group (NZ) 67 Apollo Drive, Rosedale, North Shore 0632, New Zealand

008 – 9 10 8

© Jean and Gareth Adamson MCMXCV
This edition MMIX

ISBN: 978-1-40930-056-4
Printed in China

www.topsyandtim.com

This Topsy and Tim book belongs to

_____

Topsy and Tim were having tea with Tony Welch. Tony's mum was going to have a baby. It was growing in her tummy.

Tony put his hand on his mum's big tummy.
"I can feel the baby moving," he said. Tony's
mum let Topsy and Tim feel her tummy too.
"Ooh!" said Topsy. "It kicked my hand."
"When will the baby be born?" asked Tim.
"In a week or so," said Tony's mum.
"I hope it's a girl," said Topsy.

Later, Tony took Topsy and Tim upstairs to
see the new baby's bedroom. "I'm going to let
it sleep in my old cot," he said.

Topsy and Tim had brought a bag of their old baby clothes for the new baby. They helped Tony's mum to put the clothes away in a drawer.

One morning, Tony came to school looking very pleased.
"I've got a baby brother," he told the class.
"He was born in the night and he's called Jack."
"You are lucky," said Topsy and Tim.
"Yes," said Tony. "I haven't seen him yet because he was
born in hospital but Daddy is taking me there after school."

The next day, Tony came to play with Topsy and Tim. He was carrying a new car. "Jack gave it to me," he told them. "Can we see Jack?" asked Tim.

"We'll go and meet Jack next week," said Mummy,
"when Tony's mum brings him home."
"What's he like?" asked Topsy.
"He's very little and he cries a lot," said Tony.

Topsy and Tim talked about Jack all week long.
When Saturday came, Mummy took them to see him.

"Can I hold him?" asked Topsy.
She sat on the floor and Tony's mum put him on her lap. Topsy was careful to hold the baby's head up. He felt very warm.
"I want to hold him, too," said Tim.

Jack began to cry. Tony's mum picked him up.
"Why is he crying?" asked Tim.
"Babies don't know how to talk, so they cry
when they need something," said Tony's mum.

"He's pooed his pants," said Tony.
"No, he hasn't," said his mum.
"Perhaps he's hungry," said Topsy.
"I think you're right," said Tony's mum.

Tony's mum started to feed Jack.
He stopped crying and made loud sucking noises.
"I want a drink, too," said Tony.

"There are some cartons of juice in the fridge,
Tony," said his mum. "I expect Topsy and Tim
would like a drink too."

After they'd finished their drinks,
Topsy and Tim and Tony went to
play football in the garden.

When they came back in, Tony's mum was changing
Jack's nappy. Topsy and Tim stood and watched.

"Now I'm going to give Jack his bath," said Tony's mum. "Would you like to help me, Tony?"
Tony shook his head.

Topsy and Tim played with Jack while Tony's mum
put warm water in the baby bath and tested it with
her elbow to make sure it was not too hot for Jack.

When she put Jack in the bath, he began to cry.
"He doesn't like the water," said Tim.
"Yes, he does," said Tony. He lifted the baby's
sponge and squeezed some water on to Jack's toes.

Jack stopped crying and gurgled.
"He's laughing," said Topsy.
"That's because he likes his big brother,"
said Tony's mum and she gave Tony a hug.

"Isn't Tony lucky to have a little
brother?" said Topsy on the way home.
"I think Jack's lucky to have
a big brother like Tony,"
said Tim.

*Now turn the page and help
Topsy and Tim solve a puzzle.*

Look at the toys below.
Can you find each of them
hidden in the big picture?

car

ball

duck

giraffe

pencils

teddy bear

A Map of the Town

farm

Topsy and
Tim's house

Kerry's
house

nursery
school

Tony's
house

park

garage

post office

health centre

church

primary school

police station

Look out for other titles in the series.

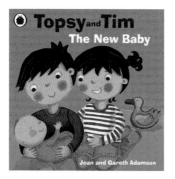

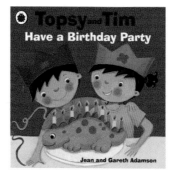

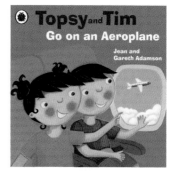

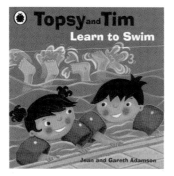

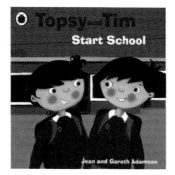

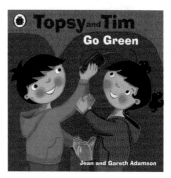

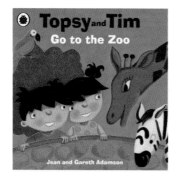

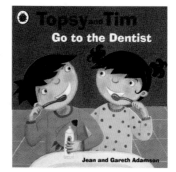